For Joan, whose surprises are always the best
—C.B.

For Brian Biggs
—G.P.

Farrar Straus Giroux Books for Young Readers
175 Fifth Avenue, New York 10010

Text copyright © 2014 by Carol Brendler • Pictures copyright © 2014 by Greg Pizzoli
All rights reserved • Color separations by Embassy Graphics Ltd. • Printed in China by RR Donnelley Asia Printing Solutions Ltd.,
Dongguan City, Guangdong Province • Designed by Elizabeth H. Clark • First edition, 2014
3 5 7 9 10 8 6 4
mackids.com
Library of Congress Cataloging-in-Publication Data
Brendler, Carol.
    Not very scary / Carol Brendler ; pictures by Greg Pizzoli. — First edition.
        pages cm
    Summary: On Halloween, Melly is invited to Cousin Malberta's home for a surprise, but as she walks there on a
beautifully spooky evening, she is followed by increasing numbers of creatures that may actually be frightening.
    ISBN 978-0-374-35547-0 (hardcover)
    [1. Halloween—Fiction.   2. Monsters—Fiction.   3. Fear—Fiction.   4. Surprises—Fiction.   5. Parties—Fiction.]
I. Pizzoli, Greg, illustrator.   II. Title.

PZ7.B7512Not 2014
[E]—dc23

                                                                                              2013011139

Farrar Straus Giroux Books for Young Readers may be purchased for business or promotional use.
For information on bulk purchases please contact Macmillan Corporate and Premium Sales
Department at (800) 221-7945 x5442 or by email at specialmarkets@macmillan.com.

NOT VERY SCARY

Carol Brendler

Pictures by
Greg Pizzoli

Farrar Straus Giroux
New York

On Halloween, Melly found this invitation in her mailbox:

MALBERTA
123 SCARY ST.
GHOST TOWN

Dear Melly,

Please come over TONIGHT. I HAVE A SURPRISE FOR YOU!

YOURS GHOULY,

COUSIN MALBERTA

Melly loved surprises and Malberta's were the best.
So on the scariest night of all, Melly set out for a visit.

The path was bleak, the air was still, and the clouds hung low and gloomy—Melly's favorite kind of weather!

But what was following her?

A coal-black cat with an itchy-twitchy tail!

"Not the least bit scary," said Melly, feeling very brave.
But then she saw . . .

. . . two skittish skeletons following one coal-black cat with an itchy-twitchy tail!

"Not quite scary," said Melly, but she shuddered from her horns to her heels.
Then she saw . . .

. . . three wheezy witches following two skittish skeletons and one coal-black cat with an itchy-twitchy tail!

"Not particularly scary," said Melly, but she bit
her claws, one by one.
Then she saw . . .

. . . four mournful ghosts following three wheezy witches, two skittish skeletons, and one coal-black cat with an itchy-twitchy tail!

"Not really scary," said Melly, but she felt the fur rise
on the scruff of her neck.
Then she saw . . .

. . . five grimy goblins following four mournful ghosts, three wheezy witches, two skittish skeletons, and one coal-black cat with an itchy-twitchy tail!

"Not remarkably scary," said Melly, but she backed away, right into a briar patch.

Then she saw . . .

. . . six sullen mummies following five grimy goblins, four mournful ghosts, three wheezy witches, two skittish skeletons, and one coal-black cat with an itchy-twitchy tail!

"Not significantly scary," said Melly, but she almost missed the turn to Malberta's.
Then she saw . . .

. . . seven frenzied fruit bats following six sullen mummies, five grimy goblins, four mournful ghosts, three wheezy witches, two skittish skeletons, and one coal-black cat with an itchy-twitchy tail!

"Not especially scary!" Melly yelled, but her little monster heart skipped a beat-beat-beat.

Then she saw . . .

. . . eight spindly spiders join seven frenzied fruit bats, six sullen mummies, five grimy goblins, four mournful ghosts, three wheezy witches, two skittish skeletons, and one coal-black cat with an itchy-twitchy tail!

"Not extraordinarily scary!" Melly yelled, but she ran and ran until she reached Malberta's place. There she saw . . .

. . . nine rambunctious rats join eight spindly spiders, seven frenzied fruit bats, six sullen mummies, five grimy goblins, four mournful ghosts, three wheezy witches, two skittish skeletons, and one coal-black cat with an itchy-twitchy tail!

"Not tremendously scary!" Melly yelled,
but she shivered as she raised the rusty latch
on the gate.
Then she saw . . .

... ten vexing vultures join nine rambunctious rats, eight spindly spiders, seven frenzied fruit bats, six sullen mummies, five grimy goblins, four mournful ghosts, three wheezy witches, two skittish skeletons, and one coal-black cat with an itchy-twitchy tail!

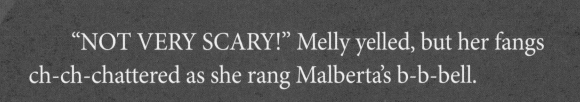

"NOT VERY SCARY!" Melly yelled, but her fangs ch-ch-chattered as she rang Malberta's b-b-bell.

"Surprise!" cried Malberta.

A party! There was poison ivy punch and lizard tongue trail mix. There was bobbing for crawdads and a Pin the Drool on the Ghoul game.

But there was no one to play with.

Where were the other party guests?

"Here we are!" shouted ten vultures, nine rats, eight spiders, seven fruit bats, six mummies, five goblins, four ghosts, three witches, two skeletons, and one coal-black cat with an itchy-twitchy tail. Malberta's friends! They were invited, too.

PIN THE
HE GH

No, they weren't very scary.

Not very scary—at all!